Holmes's face was pale. I could see that he was afraid. I had no chance to ask what had happened. Suddenly the quiet of the night was broken by a scream. It was the most terrible sound I had ever heard. It made my heart cold. They say that people heard the cry all the way down in the village.

MYSTERIES OF SHERLOCK HOLMES

Based on the stories of
Sir Arthur Conan Doyle

by **Judith Conaway**
illustrated by **Lyle Miller**

A STEPPING STONE BOOK™
Random House New York

www.steppingstonesbooks.com
www.randomhouse.com/kids

Library of Congress Cataloging-in-Publication Data
Conaway, Judith.
Mysteries of Sherlock Holmes : based on the stories of Sir Arthur Conan Doyle / by Judith Conaway ; illustrated by Lyle Miller.
    p. cm.
"A Stepping Stone Book."
SUMMARY: Amateur detective Sherlock Holmes, the master of deductive reasoning, solves several mysteries with the aid of his friend, Dr. John Watson.
ISBN 0-394-85086-6 (trade) — ISBN 0-394-95086-0 (lib. bdg.)
[1. Detective and mystery stories, American. 2. Children's stories, American. 3. Holmes, Sherlock (Fictitious character)—Juvenile literature. 4. Mystery and detective stories. 5. Short stories.] I. Doyle, Arthur Conan, Sir, 1859–1930. II. Miller, Lyle, ill. III. Title. IV. Series.
PZ7.C7575My 2005   [Fic]—dc22   2004018456

Printed in the United States of America   40 39 38 37 36 35 34 33 32 31

RANDOM HOUSE and colophon are registered trademarks and A STEPPING STONE BOOK and colophon are trademarks of Random House, Inc.

Contents

The Adventure of the Speckled Band

It was early in April 1883. At this time I was living with Sherlock Holmes. We had rooms at 221B Baker Street.

One morning I woke up early. Holmes was standing by my bed. He was already dressed. I looked up at him in surprise. My clock showed that it was only seven. Holmes got up late, as a rule.

"Very sorry to wake you up, Watson," he said.

"What is it?" I asked. "A fire?"

"No. It is a young lady. She just

came in. She says she must see me. It looks like a case, Watson. I thought you would want to be in on it from the first."

I put on my clothes. In a few minutes I was ready. We went down to the sitting room.

A lady got to her feet. She was dressed in black. We saw that her face was gray. Her eyes looked like those of a hunted animal.

"Good morning," said Holmes. "My name is Sherlock Holmes. And this is Dr. Watson. He is my dear friend. Please tell us everything."

"My name is Helen Stoner," said the lady. "I am living with my stepfather. His name is Dr. Grimesby Roylott. He is the last living Roylott. The Roylotts have been at Stoke Moran for hundreds of years."

Holmes nodded. "I know the name," said he.

Miss Stoner went on. "At one time

the Roylott family was one of the richest in England. But in the last one hundred years all has changed. Five heads of the family in a row were bad men. They did not take care of their lands. They wasted all the family's money. At last nothing was left. Nothing except a little land and a two-hundred-year-old house.

"My stepfather saw how things were. He knew he would have to make his own way. So he went to school and became a doctor. Then he went to India.

"In India, Dr. Roylott married my mother. My father had died just the year before. My twin sister, Julia, and I were only two years old when Dr. Roylott became our stepfather.

"My mother had some money—a thousand pounds a year. When she married Dr. Roylott, she made a new will. She left her money to him. The will also said that Roylott must take care of Julia and me.

"My mother died the year we came back to England. Dr. Roylott then took me and Julia to Stoke Moran. My mother's money was enough for all of us to live on. We could have had a good life.

"But after my mother died, my stepfather was a changed man. He made no friends around his old neighborhood. He would fight anyone he came across.

"Now everyone in the village is afraid of my stepfather. He is as strong as he is crazy. People stay out of his way.

"His only friends are a band of gypsies. He lets these people camp on his land. Sometimes he goes out and visits them in their tents.

"Then there are the wild animals. He brought them from India. There is a cheetah and a baboon. These two animals have the run of the place.

"From the first, my sister, Julia, and I had a very bad time. No one wanted to work at the house. We had to do all the work ourselves. Julia was only thirty when she died. But her hair was already getting white. You can see that my hair is getting white too."

"Your sister is dead, then?" Holmes asked.

"She died two years ago. It is of her death that I wish to speak. My sister and I did not get many chances to leave Stoke Moran. But we have an aunt. My stepfather let Julia and me pay short visits to her house.

"On one of those visits, my sister met a young man. She fell in love with him. They planned to marry. My stepfather said nothing against her marriage. But less than two weeks later, Julia was dead."

Sherlock Holmes had been sitting back in his chair. But at these last words he sat up. His eyes opened.

"Please give us every little fact," said he.

"That will be easy," Helen Stoner said. "Every little bit of that night will be burned into my mind for the rest of my life. As I have said, the house is very old. We live in only one wing of it. All our bedrooms are on the ground floor. The first bedroom is Dr. Roylott's. The second bedroom was my sister's. The third bedroom is mine. There are no doors between the bedrooms. But they all open out onto the same long hall.

"On the night Julia died, Dr. Roylott went to his room early. But we knew he had not gone to sleep. Julia could smell his cigars.

"Julia never could stand that smell. So she came to my room. We sat there for some time, talking about her wedding. At eleven o'clock she got up to go. But then she stopped at the door. She looked back at me.

" 'Tell me, Helen,' she said. 'Have you ever heard someone whistling in the dead of night?'

" 'Never,' said I.

" 'You're sure you don't whistle in your sleep?' she asked.

" 'No, I don't,' I said. 'Why do you ask?'

" 'I ask because I keep hearing
a whistle. I hear it about three o'clock
every morning. I am a light sleeper.
The whistle always wakes me up. I
cannot tell where the whistle is coming from. Maybe it's coming from the

next room. Maybe it's coming from outside. But I just thought I would ask if you had heard it.'

" 'No,' I said. 'I have not. Maybe it is those gypsies camping out there.'

" 'That must be it,' she said. Then she said good night. I heard her go down the hall. Then I heard her turn the key in the door."

"Hmm," said Holmes. "Did you always lock yourselves in at night?"

"Always. We were afraid of the cheetah and the baboon."

"Quite so. Please go on with your story."

"I could not sleep that night. You will remember that my sister and I were twins. They say twins can feel things that are happening to each other.

"It was a wild night. The wind was

blowing hard. The rain beat against the window.

"All of a sudden I heard a scream. It was my sister's voice! I jumped up from my bed. I ran into the hall. It was then that I heard a low whistle! A few seconds later I heard a clanging sound.

"I ran to my sister's door. It started to open. My sister came to the door. Her face was white with fear. She could not stand up.

"I ran to her. I threw my arms around her. She fell to the floor. I bent over her. Then she spoke. I will never forget her voice. 'Oh, my God, Helen!' she said. 'It was the band! The speckled band!' And then, Mr. Holmes, she died!"

"One moment," said Holmes. "Are you sure about this whistle? And

about the clanging sound? You are sure you heard them?"

"I am sure," said Helen Stoner.

"Was your sister dressed to go out?" asked Holmes.

"No. She was in her nightdress. We found a candle in her hand."

"Hmm. So she must have tried to make a light. What did the police say about the case?"

"They looked into it with great care," replied Helen Stoner. "They knew Dr. Roylott, you see. But they could not find out how Julia died. The windows were closed from the inside, with heavy bars. The walls were thick. The floor was thick too. There was no way any person could have come in the room—except through the door."

"And you are sure the door was

locked?" Holmes asked again.

Miss Stoner said that she was sure.

Holmes shook his head. I could see he was not happy. "This looks very bad," he said. "Please go on with your story."

"Two years have gone by since Julia died," said Miss Stoner. "My life has been very sad. But about a month ago a man asked me to marry him. His name is Armitage—Percy Armitage. We are going to be married this spring.

"My stepfather has said nothing against the match. But two days ago he told me that I must move into my sister's room. He said he had to fix the wall in my room. So I moved next door—into the very room in which Julia died!

"Last night I lay there, thinking

about Julia. And then I heard it! A long, low whistle! It was the same sound Julia had talked about—on the night she had died!

"I jumped up and lit a candle. I could see nothing in the room. But I could not go back to bed. I got dressed. I waited for daylight. And then I came right here, to ask your help."

Holmes said nothing for a long time. Then he spoke. "We must act right away," he said. "I will come to Stoke Moran this afternoon, Miss Stoner. Can I get into the house without Dr. Roylott knowing it?"

"Yes," she said. "He said he would be away all day."

"Good. You go back home, then," Holmes said. "We will come down on an early afternoon train."

Miss Stoner left the room.

"And what do you think of it all, Watson?" Holmes asked.

"It is a very dark business," I said.

"I am afraid it is. But we do have some clues. We have her words, 'the speckled band.' We know that a band of gypsies was camping on the land. They could have whistled. Then there was the clanging sound. That might have been a gypsy too. It could have been the clanging of a window bar."

"I see many things wrong with that idea," I said.

"So do I," said Holmes. "That is why we are going to Stoke Moran.

"Let's order breakfast, Watson. Then I shall walk downtown. I'll need some facts before we do anything else."

It was one o'clock when Holmes got back. He had a blue paper in his hand. It had notes and numbers all over it.

"I have seen the will of Dr. Roylott's wife," he said. "She left a thousand pounds, all right. But each girl was to get two hundred and fifty pounds when she got married. If the girls died before getting married, Roylott would get all the money. So you see why Dr. Roylott wanted Julia and Helen dead.

"We had better get going, Watson. And I would like it very much if you would bring your gun."

We went down to Waterloo Station. We caught the next train out. Then we found a horse and cart to take us to Stoke Moran.

Helen Stoner met us at the Stoke

Moran gate. "I have been waiting for you!" she cried.

"Don't worry," said Holmes. "We will soon get to the bottom of this. Now, please show me the house."

Helen Stoner showed us where the bedrooms were. First Holmes walked along the outside of the house. He looked at the windows. He asked Miss Stoner to go into her own room and close the windows. Then he tried to get in. He had no luck.

Next we went to the room where Julia Stoner had died. It was a small room with a low ceiling. Holmes sat down on one of the chairs. He looked the whole room over. He did not speak for a while.

"Why, here is a bellpull," he said. He pointed to a long rope on the wall. "In what part of the house does the bell ring?"

"Downstairs," Helen Stoner said. "My stepfather put it in two years ago. The bell is for calling the servants. But we never use it."

Holmes walked over to the bell-pull. He gave it a strong tug. "Why, it is a dummy," he said. "It doesn't even ring. See? It just hangs from that wire up there. The wire above the air vent.

"And by the way—what is that air vent doing up there? An air hole should go to the outside. That one seems to go into the next room. Hmm. I think I shall have a look."

We went into Dr. Roylott's room. In it were only three things. A camp bed. A wooden chair. And a large iron safe with a lamp on it.

Holmes tapped the safe. "What

is in here?" he asked.

"My stepfather's papers," replied Helen Stoner.

"Are you sure there isn't a cat in that safe?" asked Holmes. "Look at this!" He picked up a small dish of milk.

"We don't keep a cat," said Miss Stoner. "Just the cheetah and the baboon."

"This milk would not go far with a cheetah," said Holmes. "And what's this?" He held up a small dog leash. The end of it had been tied in a loop.

I have never seen my friend's face so dark. We went outside. We walked up and down the yard several times. Then Holmes spoke to Miss Stoner.

"You must do exactly as I tell you," he said. "It could mean your life." She nodded.

"See that inn across the street?" asked Holmes. "We will go there now. We will watch the house from there. Tonight I want you to go to bed in your sister's room. Just as you did last night. Then wait until you hear Dr. Roylott go to bed. At that moment open and close the window. It will be a signal to Dr. Watson and me. Then go to your own room and wait.

"Watson and I will be waiting for your signal. Then we will leave the inn. We are going to spend the night in Julia's room."

"I think you already know what happened, Mr. Holmes," said Helen Stoner. "Please tell me. How did my sister die?"

"We are not sure yet," said Holmes. "We must leave you now, Miss Stoner. We must not let the doctor see us. Until tonight, then."

Holmes and I went to the inn to wait. We had a room from which we could see Stoke Moran. At about seven we saw Dr. Roylott get home. We knew it was he. We could hear him yelling at the boy who opened the gates.

At about nine o'clock the lights in the house went out. All was dark. Two hours passed. Then we saw a light flash out from the middle window.

"That's our signal," said Holmes. A moment later we were out on the dark road. A cold wind blew in our faces. We made our way over the old stone wall and across the yard. We got in through the window of Julia's room.

We had to be very quiet. The smallest sound might wake Dr. Roylott next door. We did not dare have a light, either. Roylott might see it through the air vent. So as soon as we were safe, we blew out the candle. I had my gun ready.

"Do not go to sleep," whispered Holmes. "You may lose your life if you do."

How shall I ever forget that long wait? I could not hear a sound. We were in the dark. We heard the clock strike twelve. Then one. Then two. Then three.

Suddenly I saw a flash of light. It had come through the air vent! Then all was quiet again.

In a moment I heard another sound. It was a soft hiss. It sounded like steam coming out of a kettle. Holmes jumped up. He lit a match. He began to beat at the wall with his stick.

"You see it, Watson?" he yelled. "You see it?"

But I saw nothing. At the moment Holmes lit the match, I had heard a

low whistle. But I could not see what Holmes was hitting.

I lit the candle. Holmes's face was pale. I could see that he was afraid.

I had no chance to ask what had happened. Suddenly the quiet of the night was broken by a scream. It was the most terrible sound I had ever heard. It made my heart cold. They say that people heard the cry all the way down in the village.

"What can it mean?" I asked.

"It means that it is all over," Holmes said. "Bring your gun. We will go into Dr. Roylott's room."

A strange sight met our eyes. The lamp stood on the safe. The safe was open. In the chair next to the safe lay Dr. Roylott. The dog leash we had seen earlier was on his lap. His dead eyes looked up at the ceiling. And around his head there was a yellow band. It had brown spots on it.

"The band!" said Holmes. "The speckled band!"

The band began to move. It lifted its head. It was a snake!

"It is a swamp adder. The most dangerous snake in India," said Holmes.

"Let's put it back in its cage."

Holmes picked up the dog leash. He looped it around the snake's head. He carried the snake to the safe and closed the door.

This story is getting too long. So I will not say too much about how we broke the news to poor Helen Stoner. Or about how we took her to her aunt's house. Or about how the police said that Dr. Roylott had died by accident. They said he had been playing with a dangerous pet.

Holmes filled me in on his side of the case. "As soon as I saw that bell-pull, I knew," he said. "It was there for some reason. It did not ring the bell. So it must have something to do with that air vent. Then I remembered. Helen Stoner had said that Julia could smell cigar smoke. So that air vent must go into Dr. Roylott's room!

"Dr. Roylott had a cheetah and a baboon. Why not a snake too? I was doubly sure as soon as I saw the dish of milk. Roylott had trained the snake to crawl through the vent and down the rope. The snake would come back when he whistled! The clang that Helen heard? That was the safe door closing.

"I knew the doctor would try the snake trick again. This time Helen would be killed. So I waited. When I heard the snake hiss, I hit."

"You drove the snake back into

the other room," said I.

"Yes," said Holmes. "I hit the snake so hard it was good and mad. So it turned on its owner. In a way, I was the one who made Dr. Roylott die."

Holmes sighed and picked up his pipe. "I cannot say that I am very sorry," he said.

The Red-headed League

Sherlock Holmes still lives in our old rooms at 221B Baker Street. I called upon him there one day last fall.

I found Holmes deep in talk. With him was a fat old man who had bright red hair.

"Come in, Dr. Watson!" Holmes cried. "Meet Mr. J. B. Wilson. Mr. Wilson, this is Dr. Watson. He works with me on many of my cases."

The fat man got up and made me a little bow. Holmes sat back. He put his fingers together. (He often does that when he is thinking.) He smiled.

"Watson, my dear man, I know you love strange stories as much as I do. Mr. Wilson here has just started telling his tale. And it's one of the strangest stories I have ever heard."

Mr. Wilson looked proud. He pulled a piece of paper out of his coat pocket. "Look at this notice, Dr. Watson," he said. "You may read it for yourself."

I took the paper from him.

To All Red-headed Men

There is a job open at the Red-headed League. The pay is 4 pounds a week. The work is not very hard. To get the job you must have red hair. You must be a man over 21 years old. Come in person on Monday, at 11 o'clock, to 7 Fleet Street. Ask for Duncan Ross.

"What can it mean?" I asked.

Holmes gave a chuckle. "It IS a little odd, isn't it? Do tell us more, Mr. Wilson."

"I own a store at Coburg Square," said Wilson. "It's a very small place. Of late years it has not done much more than give me a living. I used to have two helpers. Now I can pay only one. I can pay him only because he will work for half pay. I don't know what I would do without him."

"Hmm. A good helper who works for half pay," said Holmes. "And what is the name of this nice young man?"

"Vincent Spaulding," replied Wilson. "Oh, Vincent does have his problems. He is always down in the basement. He plays with all those cameras of his down there. A real photo nut. But on the whole he's a very good worker.

"One day about eight weeks ago, Spaulding came into my room. He had this paper in his hand. 'I tell you, Mr. Wilson,' Spaulding said, 'I wish I were a red-headed man. Here's another job open at the Red-headed League.'

"Now, I had never heard of the Red-headed League. I don't get out too much. But Spaulding knew all about it.

"He told me that the league had been started by Ezekiah Hopkins. Hopkins was an American millionaire. He had bright red hair.

"All his life people made fun of Hopkins because of his red hair. Then Hopkins came to London. In London he got rich. So he loved London. And he felt sorry for men with red hair. So when he died, Hopkins left his money to the red-headed men of London.

"Now, as you may have noticed, my hair is very red. So it was easy for Spaulding to talk me into giving the job a try. 'What have you got to lose?' he asked me.

"That was a Monday. It's always a slow day at the store. So we shut the shop. Spaulding went with me to Fleet Street.

"I never saw such a sight. Fleet Street was packed with red-headed men. The street looked like a wagon full of oranges. I saw every shade of red you can think of. Orange red. Brick red. Irish setter red.

"I was ready to give up and go home. But Spaulding would not hear of it. I do not know how he did it. But he pushed and pulled. At last he got me to the door.

"We joined the line going up the steps. There was another line of men coming down. They were men who had been turned down.

"Our line kept moving. Soon we found ourselves in a room on the second floor. There was nothing in the room except two chairs and a table. Behind the table sat a small man. His hair was as red as mine. This man looked over each new job hunter. He found some small reason to say no to each one.

"But my turn was different. The red-headed man took one look at me. Then he got up and closed the door. He shook my hand. 'I'm Duncan Ross,' he said.

"I was too afraid to say anything. So my helper spoke for me. 'This is J. B. Wilson,' said Spaulding. 'He's here about the job with the Red-headed League.'

" 'And he's just right for it!' cried Duncan Ross. 'I don't think I have ever seen such a fine head of hair.'

"Ross stepped over to the open window. 'The job has been taken!' he shouted. One by one the men below all went away. Soon Mr. Duncan Ross and I were the only redheads in sight.

"Ross turned to me. 'How soon can you start your new job?'

" 'Uh, I don't know . . .' said I. 'You see, I have a small store—'

"Vincent Spaulding broke in. 'Oh, don't worry about the store, Mr. Wilson,' he said. 'I can take care of that for you.'

"So I said I would work for Mr. Ross. I was to come to Fleet Street every day between ten and two. My job? Well, you are not going to believe this. All I had to do was to copy the *Encyclopedia Britannica*. That's all. And for that I would be paid four pounds a week!

"I walked out of there feeling very pleased with myself. But not for long. Quite soon I began having second thoughts. This all had to be some kind of joke. I just couldn't believe that story about Ezekiah Hopkins.

"But as my helper had said, I had nothing to lose. So I showed up at Fleet Street the next day at ten.

"To my surprise, everything went just as Mr. Ross had said it would. I went to Fleet Street every day. I copied the encyclopedia. Every Saturday Mr. Ross would come in and pay me four pounds.

"Things went on this way for eight weeks. I copied out all the facts about animals. About apples. About Africa. I began to get tired of the A's. I hoped to finish soon and get on to the B's. Then all at once the whole business came to an end."

"What? To an end?" asked Sherlock Holmes.

"Yes, sir," said Wilson. "It happened only this morning. I went to work at ten o'clock. When I got there I found this card on the door."

The Red-headed League no longer exists.
October 9, 1890

Sherlock Holmes and I read this card. We looked at J. B. Wilson's face. The funny side of his story made us forget ourselves. We laughed until we roared.

"I can't see that it's very funny,"

cried Mr. Wilson. His face turned as
red as his hair. "If you're going to
make fun of me, I'll leave."

"No, no. Don't go," said Holmes.
"I very much want to hear your

47

story. I have a feeling it could be something very important."

"Why, of course it's important," said Mr. Wilson. "I have lost four pounds a week!"

"Come, come, Mr. Wilson," said Holmes. "You have lost nothing. You are thirty-two pounds richer than you thought you would be. To say nothing of what you now know about things starting with A."

"But I want to know what it was all about!" Mr. Wilson said. "That's why I came to you, Mr. Holmes. Can you find out for me?"

"I will do my best," said Holmes. "But first—a question. This Vincent Spaulding. This helper of yours. What does he look like?"

"Well, he's small. But very quick and strong. About thirty years old.

He has a patch of very white skin on his face."

Holmes sat up straight. He was very excited. "That's enough, Mr. Wilson," he said. "You may go home now. Today is Saturday. By Monday I will have your answer."

When Wilson had gone, Holmes turned to me. "Well, Watson," he asked. "What do you make of it?"

"I make nothing of it," I answered. "It is very strange. What are you going to do?"

"Go hear some music," replied Holmes. "There is a violin concert at St. James's Hall this afternoon. Come along. We have time to make a stop on the way."

We took the underground train to Aldersgate. A short walk, and we were in Coburg Square.

One of the corner houses wore a sign that read "J. B. Wilson." Holmes stopped in front of the house. He thumped on the sidewalk with his stick. He pounded in two or three more spots. Then he walked up and knocked on the door.

Mr. Wilson's helper answered. He was a bright, clean looking young man.

"So sorry to bother you," said Holmes. "But can you tell me how to get to the Strand?"

"Third right, fourth left," the young man answered. He closed the door.

"That," said Holmes as we walked away, "is the fourth smartest man in London. I have come across him before. Did you get a look at his knees?"

"What about his knees?" I asked.

"What do you know, Holmes? Why did you pound the sidewalk like that?"

"My dear doctor," said Holmes. "This is no time to talk. This is the time to look. Let's see what lies behind this quiet block." We turned the corner.

To my surprise, we found ourselves on a busy street. "Let's see," said Holmes. "There's a cigar store. And there's the City Bank. And there is a restaurant. Hmm, yes . . ."

He turned to me. "I'll want your help," he said. "Can you be ready at ten tonight? Good. See you then. Oh, and Dr. Watson. Do you have your gun? You had better bring it along."

He waved his hand. Then he disappeared.

I got back to Baker Street just before ten o'clock that evening. Two horse-drawn cabs were waiting outside. Inside, I found two men with Holmes.

"Ah! We are all here now!" Holmes said. "You know Inspector Jones of Scotland Yard, don't you, Watson? And this is Mr. Merryweather."

Mr. Merryweather was long, thin, and sad-faced. He wore a very shiny top hat. He did not look at all happy. "This had better not be a wild-goose chase," he said. "I'm missing my Saturday night card game. First time in twenty years."

Holmes laughed. "You'll play a more exciting game tonight," he said. "You, Mr. Merryweather, stand to win or lose thirty thousand pounds.

And you, Mr. Jones? You stand to get your man."

"That's right!" cried Inspector Jones. "John Clay. Killer. Robber. He's a young man. But he's at the top of the crime heap.

"Yes—he's quite a man, John Clay. The grandson of a duke. Went to the high-class schools. His head is as quick as his fingers. I've been on his trail for years. I've never even set eyes on him yet."

"I hope you will meet him to-night," said Holmes. "Let's go. Two cabs are waiting outside. You two men take the first cab. Dr. Watson and I will follow in the second."

Holmes did not say much during the long drive. We drove through the dark streets. Soon we got to the busy street near Mr. Wilson's house.

Merryweather and Jones were there ahead of us. We followed Mr. Merryweather down a narrow alley. There was a side door there. He opened it. Inside was a small hall. At the end of the hall there was a heavy gate. Merryweather opened that too. Then we went down some narrow stone stairs. There was another heavy gate at the bottom.

Merryweather stopped to light a lamp. He opened the gate and we passed into a large room. It was piled with boxes.

Holmes held the lamp up to the roof. "Looks as if no one can get in from above," he said.

"Or from below," added Merryweather. He tapped the floor with his cane. "Why—dear me! It sounds hollow!" he cried.

"Quiet now!" whispered Holmes. "Please sit down on one of these boxes. And do try not to get in the way. Your shouting has already put us in danger."

Merryweather looked hurt. But he sat down.

"We have at least an hour to wait," Holmes said. "They will do nothing until our red-haired friend is in bed. After that they will not lose a minute.

"By now, Dr. Watson, I'm sure you know where we are," Holmes went on. "We are in a room under the City Bank. Mr. Merryweather here is the head of the bank. I'll let him tell you why John Clay will soon enter this basement."

"It is our French gold," the banker whispered. "Over thirty thousand pounds' worth." He bit his nails and looked sad. "We were afraid something like this would happen."

"Don't worry," said Holmes. "It will all be over soon. And now we must cover the lamp. I'm afraid we will have to wait in the dark. But first let's get in place. These are very dangerous men. We will have to be careful. I will hide behind this box. You men hide over there. Wait till I flash the light. Then close in on them. Watson, keep your gun ready. If they fire, shoot them down in their tracks."

I bent down behind a wooden box. I kept my gun hand on top of the box. I was ready for anything.

How long that wait seemed! Later I learned that we had waited only an hour and a quarter. But it felt like all night. I tried not to move. I was afraid to make a sound. I could hear the other men breathing.

Suddenly my eyes caught a flash of light on the floor. The flash got larger. It became a yellow line. Then a hole opened. A hand came out of the hole. It was a thin, white hand.

The hand felt the floor around the hole. Then everything went dark again.

But not for long. There was a tearing sound. The hole in the floor got bigger. Over the edge peeped the face of a young man. There was a patch of bright white skin on his forehead. The young man pulled himself up into the room.

A second later he pulled a second young man up. The second man was also small and thin. He had a pale face. His hair was bright, bright red.

At that second Sherlock Holmes flashed the light.

"Great Scott!" yelled the first man. "Jump, Archie!"

"It's no use, John Clay," said Holmes. "You have no chance at all."

Inspector Jones had the handcuffs ready.

"Don't you touch me with your dirty hands," said John Clay. "I have

noble blood, you know." The cuffs closed around his wrists.

"You see it all now, Watson," said Holmes. It was early the next morning. We were back at Baker Street drinking tea. "There was only one reason for the Red-headed League. That was to get our old friend Mr. Wilson out of his store. You may think it was an odd way to do it. But I can hardly think of a better one.

"Of course what gave them the idea was Mr. Wilson's red hair. By chance it happened to be the same color as Archie's hair. So Archie became . . ."

"Mr. Duncan Ross!" I cried.

"Quite so. And John Clay became Vincent Spaulding. Remember how he was always in the basement? He said it was for photography. But I knew better as soon as I saw his knees. They were dirty. It was proof that he had been digging.

"Then I tapped the sidewalk in front of the house. No—he wasn't digging out that way. So he must be digging toward the back of the house. We walked around the block. And there I saw the City Bank."

Suddenly Holmes laughed. "Do you know what a red herring is, Dr. Watson? It's a false clue that is meant to lead us away from the real clues. Well, you've got to hand it to John Clay. He's not only smart. He's funny. Don't you get it? The Red-headed League was just a red hair-ing, all along!"

The Adventure
of the Blue Carbuncle

It was the second morning after Christmas. I called on my friend Sherlock Holmes to give him good wishes for the holiday.

I found the great detective lying on the sofa. He was smoking his favorite pipe. Next to the sofa stood a chair. On the chair's back there hung a black hat. The hat was dirty and torn.

A magnifying glass lay on the seat of the chair. Holmes had been looking at the hat.

"You know Peterson, the doorman?" asked Holmes.

"Yes," said I.

"He found this hat. He brought it here this morning—along with a good, fat goose. Right now the goose is cooking over Peterson's fire.

"The facts are these. It was four o'clock on Christmas morning. Peterson was walking home late. He had been at a little party. Peterson could see a man walking ahead of him in the gaslight. He was a tall man. He carried a white goose over his shoulder.

"The tall man got to the corner of Goodge Street. Just then a gang of toughs came into the street. One of the toughs knocked off the tall man's hat. The tall man tried to fight back with his stick. Instead, he broke the window behind him.

"Peterson rushed up to help the

tall stranger. But at the sound of the
breaking glass, the man dropped the
goose and ran. The gang of roughs
ran away too. So Peterson was left
with the goose—and this hat."

"Which, surely, he gave back to the owner?" asked I.

"My dear fellow. There lies the problem. True, we know the NAME of the owner. See? Here's a small card that was tied to the left leg of the goose. The card says, 'For Mrs. Henry Baker.' Then, here are the letters 'H. B.' inside the hat. So we're pretty sure the tall man was Henry Baker. But there are thousands of people named Baker in London. And HUNDREDS of them must be named Henry.

"Well, Peterson brought the hat to me. He kept the goose as long as he could. But today it had to be cooked or it would spoil. So Peterson took the goose home. He left the hat for me."

At that moment the door flew

open. Peterson, the doorman, rushed into the room. His face was red.

"The goose, Mr. Holmes! The goose, sir!" he gasped.

"What about it?" asked Holmes.

"See here, sir! See what my wife found inside!" He held out his hand. There lay a shining blue stone. It was no bigger than a bean in size. But it was so pure and bright that it twinkled like a star.

Sherlock Holmes sat up with a whistle. "By Jove, Peterson!" said he. "This is a treasure indeed. I suppose you know what you have there?"

"Not the Countess of Morcar's blue carbuncle!" I broke in.

"The very same," Holmes replied. "I ought to know this stone's size and shape. Haven't I been reading about it in *The Times* every single day? The

countess says she will give whoever finds it a thousand pounds."

"If I remember rightly," I put in, "the countess lost the stone at the Hotel Cosmopolitan."

"That's right," said Holmes. "It was on December twenty-second— just five days ago. The police have arrested a plumber named John Horner. I have the story here, I think."

He found the page he was looking for. He read the news story out loud.

Jewel Robbery at Hotel Cosmopolitan

John Horner, a plumber, was arrested today. The police say he stole a jewel from the jewel case of the Countess of Morcar. The jewel is known as the blue carbuncle.

Horner was arrested because of a story told by James Ryder. Ryder works for the hotel. Ryder said that he took Horner to the Countess of Morcar's room to fix a pipe. That was on the very day of the robbery.

Ryder stayed in the room for a while. But he was called away. Horner was left in the room alone.

When Ryder got back, Horner was nowhere around. But the dresser had been forced open. A jewel box was lying on the dressing table. The box was empty.

The police say that Horner put up a fight when he was arrested. "I didn't do it!" Horner had cried. But Horner had once served time for robbery. So the judge put him in jail while the Court waited for proof. When Horner heard that he was not free, he fainted.

"Hmm," said Holmes. "So much

for what the police know." He threw the paper to one side. "Well, well, Watson! The question now is this: How did the stone get out of the box and into the bird?

"Here is the stone. The stone came from the goose. The goose came from Henry Baker. So now, we must set ourselves to find Henry Baker.

"Give me a pencil, please. And that slip of paper." Holmes wrote this note:

Found. At the corner of Goodge Street, a goose and a black felt hat. Mr. Henry Baker can have the same by coming to 221B Baker Street at 6:30 this evening.

"There. That's clear." Holmes handed the paper to the doorman. "Here, Mr. Peterson. Please see that this note is put in all the evening papers. The *Globe.* The *Star.* The *Evening News.* The *Echo.* And any other newspapers you can think of."

"Very well, sir," said Peterson. "And the stone?"

"Ah, yes. I will keep the stone. Thank you. And, I say, Peterson— just buy a goose on the way back. We must have another bird to take the place of the one your family is now eating."

After Peterson left, Holmes picked up the stone. He held it against the light. "It's a bonny thing," he said. "Just see how it glints and sparkles. Of course it makes crimes happen. Every good stone does."

"Do you think this man Horner took the stone?" I asked.

"I cannot tell," replied Holmes.

"What about Henry Baker?" I went on.

"I think Henry Baker probably had nothing to do with it," Holmes said. "But I shall find out for sure as soon as Henry Baker answers my ad. Until then, I can do nothing."

"In that case," said I, "I shall keep going on my rounds. I have sick people to visit. I'll come back tonight, if I may. I'd like to see how this all will end."

"I'll be glad to see you," said Holmes. "Stay for dinner at seven."

It was six thirty before I found myself back in Baker Street. As I got near the house, I saw a tall man waiting. The tall man and I entered together.

Holmes rose from his seat. "Mr. Henry Baker, I believe," he said.

"Please take this chair by the fire. You look cold. Ah, Watson, you have just come at the right time. Is that your hat, Mr. Baker?"

"Yes, sir. It is my hat."

"About the bird," Holmes went on. "I'm sorry, but we had to eat it."

"To eat it!" Mr. Baker half rose from his chair. He was very upset.

"Yes. The bird would have spoiled had we NOT eaten it. But here is another goose instead. It is about the same size as the other. Won't it do just as well?"

"Oh, of course, of course," said Mr. Baker.

Sherlock Holmes looked at me. I could tell Mr. Baker had passed the test. It was clear that he knew nothing about the jewel.

"There is your hat, then. And

there is your bird," said Holmes. "By the way, could you tell me where the other goose came from? I have never tasted a better goose."

"It came from the Alpha Inn," Baker replied. "I go there almost every night. This year the owner started a goose club. My friends and I gave a few pennies each week. Then at Christmas we each got a goose. The rest of the story you know. I thank you very much, Mr. Holmes, for all you have done."

Mr. Baker bowed to us and went on his way. Holmes closed the door after him. "So much for Henry Baker. Are you hungry, Watson?"

"Not very," I answered.

"Then let's save dinner until later. We can follow up this clue while it is still hot."

It was a bitter-cold night. We put on our overcoats and wrapped up our throats. Outside the stars were shining coldly in a cloudless sky. Our breaths looked like smoke. Our steps rang sharply on the pavement.

Fifteen minutes later we were at the Alpha Inn. Holmes asked for two glasses of beer. The owner brought them to us.

"Your beer should be wonderful if it is as good as your geese," said Holmes to the owner.

"My geese?"

"Yes. I was talking just a while ago to Mr. Henry Baker. He was in your goose club, I think."

"Ah, yes! I see. But you see, sir, them's not OUR geese. I got two dozen of them from a man named Breckinridge. He sells meat over at Covent Garden."

"I thank you," said Holmes. "Here's to your health, sir. Good night."

We went out again into the frosty air. "Now for Mr. Breckinridge," Holmes said as he buttoned his coat.

We zigzagged through the back streets. Soon we were in the Covent Garden market. We saw the name

Breckinridge on one of the largest stalls. The owner was a horsey looking man. He had a sharp face. He and a small boy were just closing up.

"Good evening. It's a cold night," said Holmes. "You are sold out of geese, I see."

"I can let you have five hundred geese in the morning," the man replied.

"That won't do," said Holmes. "I want the same kind of geese you sold to the Alpha Inn. They were fine birds. Where did you get them?"

To my surprise, the question made Breckinridge angry.

"Now then, mister," he said. "What is all this about? I haven't heard anything else all day. 'Where did you get all the geese? Who did you sell the geese to?' You would

think they were the only geese in the world. People are making such a fuss about them."

"Well, I have nothing to do with the others who have been asking," Holmes said. He sounded as if he did not care very much about it. "You won't tell us. So we'll have to call off the bet. You see, I've bet five pounds those Alpha Inn geese were raised in the country."

"Then you will lose," said Breckinridge. "Those geese were raised here in town."

"You'll never make me believe that."

"Will you bet, then?" Breckinridge asked.

"That would just be stealing your money," answered Holmes. "But I'll take you on."

Breckinridge laughed. He called the small boy to his side. "Bring me the books, Bill," said he.

"Now, then, Mr. Know-It-All," he went on. "You see this little book? This is the list of folks from whom I buy. The numbers tell where to find them in the big book. See this page? It's in black ink. Those are my country goose-raisers. See this list in red? Those are my town people. Now, look at that third name. Just read it to me."

Holmes read. "Mrs. Oakshott, 117 Brixton Road. Number 249."

"Quite so. Now look up that number in this big book."

Holmes turned a page. "Here you are. Mrs. Oakshott, 117 Brixton Road. Eggs and Birds."

"Now," said Breckinridge. "What

is the last thing it says there? 'December twenty-second. Twenty-four geese. At seven and a half shillings. Sold to the Alpha Inn at twelve shillings.'

"Well? What do you say now?" Breckinridge asked.

Holmes turned red. He took a coin from his pocket. He threw it down on the table. He turned away with an air of disgust.

We walked a little way down the street. Then Holmes began laughing to himself. "I saw a horse-racing form in that man's pocket," he said. "You can always use a bet with a man like that. It's the sure way to get what you want. We are near the end, Watson. Let's go home for dinner. We can visit Mrs. Oakshott tomorrow."

Just then there were shouts behind

us. We turned. There was trouble back in Mr. Breckinridge's stall! Breckinridge was yelling at a little rat-faced man. "I've had enough of you and your geese!" he shouted. "I wish you were all dead. Get away or I'll set the dog on you! Get out! Out!"

"Ha! This may save us that visit to Mrs. Oakshott tomorrow!" said Holmes. "Come, Watson. Let's see who this fellow is."

Holmes and I walked fast. Soon we were right behind the little man. Holmes touched the man's back. He jumped. His face turned white. "Who are you? What do you want?" he cried.

"Excuse me," said Holmes. "But I couldn't help hearing your questions about the geese. I believe I can help you."

"Who are you? And how can you know anything of this?"

"My name is Sherlock Holmes. It is my business to know things. I know you're looking for a goose. The goose was grown by a Mrs. Oakshott. It was then sold to Breckinridge. He in turn sold the goose to the Alpha Inn. The owner of the Alpha sold the goose to a Mr. Henry Baker."

"Oh, sir, you're just the person I need!" the little man cried.

"In that case, come over to my place," said Holmes. "It's better to be warm while we talk. Before we go, will you tell me your name?"

The man looked to one side. "John Robinson," he said.

"No, no, the REAL name," Holmes said sweetly.

Red spots came into the man's white face. "Well, then," said he. "My real name is James Ryder."

"That's right," said Holmes. "You work at the Hotel Cosmopolitan. Step into this cab, Mr. Ryder. I shall soon be able to tell you everything you want to know."

The little man looked at Holmes. He was not sure if this was wonderful or terrible. At last he got in. Half an hour later we were back in Baker Street. Not one word had been said during our drive.

"Here we are!" said Holmes cheerily. "That fire looks very nice. You look cold, Mr. Ryder. Please take that chair by the fire. I'll just put on my slippers. . . . Now! You want to know what happened to your goose?"

"Oh yes, sir!"

"It came here. And quite a goose it was too. I don't wonder that you want to know about it. It laid an egg, after it was dead. The brightest little blue egg that ever was seen. I have it here."

Holmes opened his safe. He held

up the blue carbuncle. It shone out like a star. Ryder stared. He did not move.

"The game's up, Ryder," said Holmes quietly.

At that, Ryder started to faint. "Help him to his chair, Watson!" cried Holmes. "Give him a dash of brandy! There. He's starting to come to."

The brandy brought some color back to the man's face. "I know almost everything," said Holmes.

"Your plan was pretty low, wasn't it? You knew Horner had once served time in jail. So you knew the police would pick him up first. So what did you do? You made up some small job in the countess's room. Then you sent Horner in to do it. When Horner was done, you took the jewel. Then you called the police. Then you—"

Ryder threw himself on the rug. "Don't turn me in!" he begged. "I have never done wrong before."

"Get back into your chair!" said Holmes. "It's all very well for you to be sorry now. But you thought nothing of sending Mr. Horner to prison."

"I'll leave England, Mr. Holmes."

"Hum! We will talk about that," Holmes said. "But now let's have it. How did the stone get into the goose? How did the goose get sold? Tell us the truth, man. It's your only hope."

Ryder licked his lips. "I will tell you how it happened," said he. "The police arrested Horner. But I knew I must get the stone away at once. At any time the police might search me. There was no safe place in the hotel.

"So I made for my sister's place.

She is married to a man named Oak-shott. She raises geese for market.

"All the way to my sister's, I thought every man I met was a policeman. It was a cold night. But sweat was running down my face. My sister said I looked sick. I took my pipe and went out into the yard. I wondered what would be best to do.

"I made up my mind to go to Kilburn. I knew a man there. Name of Maudsley. He went to the bad and has just served time. I knew Maudsley could help me sell the jewel.

"But how could I be safe? The police might stop me at any moment. They would find the stone on me. I stood looking down at the geese. Then the idea came to me.

"My sister had promised me the pick of her geese for my Christmas present. I would have my goose now. And that's how I would carry the stone to Kilburn!

"I caught one of the geese. It was a fine big white one, with a bar on its tail. I took it to the back of the yard. I opened its beak. The bird put up a fight. But I got the stone into it.

"Just then the goose jumped from my arms. It ran back to the others. And I had to catch it again.

"I walked all the way to Kilburn with the goose. My pal laughed until he choked at what I had done. Then we cut open the goose. My heart turned to water. There was no sign of the stone! I knew there had been some terrible mistake.

"I ran back to my sister's. There was not a goose in sight! My sister had taken them all to market. She

had sold them to Breckinridge."

" 'Was there another goose like the one I killed?' I asked her.

" 'Oh, yes,' she replied. 'There were two geese with bars on their tails. I never could tell them apart.'

"Well—you know the rest."

Ryder suddenly began to cry.

There was a long silence. It was broken only by the sound of Holmes's fingers, tapping. Then my friend got up. He threw open the door.

"Get out!" said he.

"What, sir? Oh, bless you!"

"No more words. Get out!"

And no more words were needed. There was a crash on the stairs. Then a door banged. Then we heard footsteps running away.

Holmes reached for his pipe. "I look at it this way, Watson," he said. "The police do not pay me to do their work. The countess will have her toy. The case against Horner can go nowhere unless Ryder speaks against him.

"That man will not go wrong again. He is too afraid. Send him to jail now and you make him a jailbird for life. Besides, it is the season to forgive.

"Now I think it's time we looked into another bird. Let's hope our dinner won't start us on another wild-goose chase."

Judith Conaway is a full-time freelance writer and all-around creative person. She specializes in writing educational and audiovisual materials and is the author of Random House's four Funny Face reading workbooks. She is also a weaver, a puppet maker, and the author of three craft books. Ms. Conaway lives in New York City.

Lyle Miller has been illustrating juvenile books for the past ten years while also doing advertising and magazine work. *Mysteries of Sherlock Holmes* is his first book for Random House. Mr. Miller lives in Oklahoma City, Oklahoma.